BLITZ KIDS

Written by Jim Eldridge

Illustrated by Monica Auriemma

Collins

Chapter 1

BOOOOMMMMM!!!!

The bomb landed in the next street, but it seemed to 12-year-old Ellie Smith as if it was right next to her. She was standing with her nine-year-old brother, Sammy, holding his hand, when she heard a whining noise from the sky. The next moment the ground rose up around her, throwing her into the air, and she was lying on the pavement, dust and smoke all around her. Ellie was aware of the heavy drone of the bombers overhead and the bone-penetrating scream of the air-raid siren.

"Sammy!" she yelled.

She could hardly see because of all the smoke
and dust. Ellie heard a crying sound and reached out,
and felt Sammy lying on the pavement.

"I'm scared …" Sammy whimpered. "I'm going
to die."

"You're not going to die," Ellie told him.
She didn't know if it was true, but she felt she had to
say something.

Sammy stumbled to his feet. Ellie hung on to his arm, as she didn't want to lose him. Both of them were covered in thick dust. Ellie wished her mum was here. And then suddenly, she was.

"Ellie!" she heard her shout, and then her mum had hold of Ellie. In her other hand, she was holding on to Ellie's six-year-old brother, Micky.

"I told you to get to the shelter!" she yelled angrily.

"We were waiting for you," Ellie said.

Chapter 2

They reached the tube station as another bomb exploded not far away, shaking the pavement beneath their feet. Ellie held on to Sammy and their mum held Micky's hand, as they hurried down the winding stairs to the platforms deep beneath the ground. They made their way through the crowd of people until they found their next-door neighbour, Mrs Watson, who had reserved a space for them. She'd spread blankets and scattered cushions for them to sit down on. Some people had brought chairs with them, and one family even had a couple of mattresses so they could sleep lying down.

"The bombing's started early tonight," said Mrs Watson. "I barely had time to find my gas mask before the first one dropped. Have you got yours?"

Ellie showed her the box that contained her gas mask, and Sammy and Micky did the same.

Sammy and Micky lay down on the cushions. It was well past their bedtime and they were both ready to sleep. Ellie found sleeping difficult, aware of the bombs falling outside and worried if their house would still be standing when they left after the all clear sounded, which was usually when dawn was coming.

Ellie had found sleeping hard ever since the war started the year before, when she'd been evacuated to the countryside, along with all the other children in London. This was because everyone expected the Germans to start bombing London as soon as the war started. Ellie, Sammy and Micky and over three million other children were packed into trains and coaches without their parents and taken far away to parts of the country that the government didn't think would be bombed. In fact, the bombing hadn't really started until just a few weeks ago.

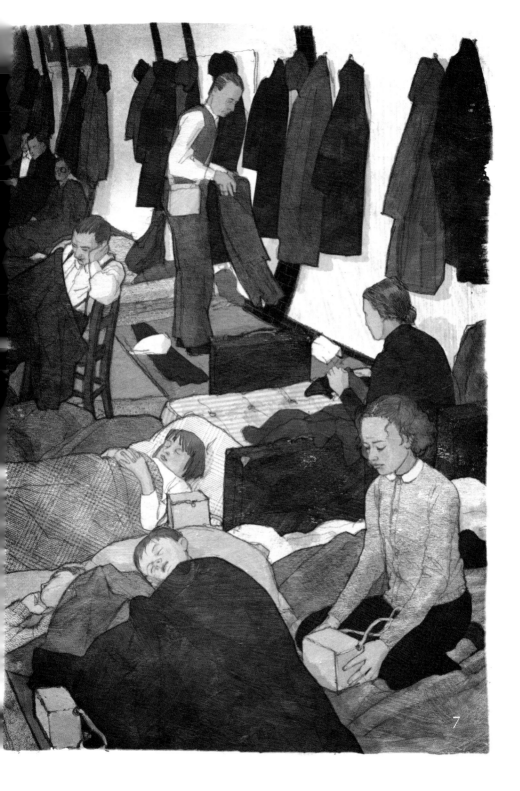

Ellie hadn't slept at all after she'd been evacuated. Nor had Sammy and Micky. The three of them had been placed with a miserable couple, Mr and Mrs Rudd, who wanted them to do all the hard and dirty work in the house while their own children just lazed around. Ellie had complained that it was unfair, but Mr and Mrs Rudd just shouted at them and told them if they didn't work, they wouldn't get any food.

After two months of this misery, Ellie managed to smuggle a letter to her mum telling her how bad things were, and their mum actually turned up and said she was taking her children back to London! Ellie was overjoyed to be going home, but that good feeling was dashed when they got back to London. Ellie was heartbroken to find her dad had joined up in the army and was now away fighting in France.

Every day, Ellie listened to the news on the wireless to find out what was happening in the war, hoping she'd hear that her dad would be coming home. Instead, the news was bad. The British army had been pushed back by the Germans to a place called Dunkirk in northern France, and the soldiers were trapped there, about half a million of them. Ellie didn't know if her dad was among them.

It felt like forever before they heard the good news that he'd been rescued, along with a third of a million soldiers, taken off the beaches by small boats while under attack from German tanks, big heavy guns and aircraft.

Ellie had never been so glad to see her dad walking up the street to their house in his uniform, and she and her mum and Sammy and Micky rushed out to greet him, throwing themselves at him and hugging him tight. Dad didn't say much about how things had been at Dunkirk; said he'd prefer not to think about it.

As it was, he wasn't home for very long. About a week after he came back from Dunkirk, he was off again. This time he was being sent to Egypt. Ellie didn't know where Egypt was, so she looked it up in an atlas and found it was a country in north Africa, a very hot country that was mostly desert.

Ellie was desperate to tell her dad she didn't want him to go. She wanted him to stay at home with them.

But her dad said it was his duty to go to defend
the country and his family. If he didn't, the Germans
would win and they'd all be prisoners under
the control of Adolf Hitler, who was a dictator.
So instead Ellie hugged him and kissed him goodbye
when it was time for him to leave. But for weeks after
he'd gone, she didn't sleep properly; she kept waking
up worrying if he was all right, or if he was being shot
at and bombed, like at Dunkirk.

And then came the Battle of Britain, when
the Germans sent thousands of huge planes over to
bomb the airfields in Kent and Sussex.

Mrs Watson told Ellie this was so the RAF wouldn't be able to defend Britain when the Germans launched their invasion. She'd been told this by her son, who worked for the government. For weeks, Ellie didn't sleep properly after days spent looking up at the skies and seeing the small British fighter planes, Spitfires and Hurricanes, attacking the big German bombers. Thousands of bombs came down, badly damaging towns and airfields, but so many of the German bomber planes were shot down that in the end the Germans gave up these daytime raids.

Instead, they began to send the bombers over at nighttime because the small British fighter planes couldn't fly so well in darkness. For the last two weeks, the German bombers had been attacking London, so there was even less chance of Ellie getting a good night's sleep. And not just London. From the news on the wireless, Ellie learnt that other cities were being bombed: Birmingham, Belfast, Manchester, Glasgow, Hull, Bristol, Cardiff, Portsmouth, Sheffield and loads of others.

Mrs Watson said the Germans called it a Blitzkrieg; at least that's what her son told her. For everyone in Britain, it was just the Blitz. Ellie and her mum and brothers hardly went to bed at home any more in the evenings. Instead, they stayed up waiting for the high-pitched wail of the air-raid warning, at which they would grab their gas masks and whatever they could and head for the tube station.

"You ought to try and get some sleep, Ellie," said her mum, and she patted the cushions and blanket beside her. "Come on."

"I'll sleep in a minute, Mum," said Ellie. "You put your head down. I'll be all right."

She looked along the platform. It was midnight and nearly everyone on the platform was asleep, either lying down or sitting in chairs. Just a few people like her were still awake.

We're the nervous ones, thought Ellie. *The worried.* And she marvelled at those, like her mum and Mrs Watson who were able to sleep while above them the bombs were falling.

How can they sleep? she wondered.

Chapter 3

The next morning, the sound of the all-clear echoed through the tube station. Most people were already awake and were queuing to use the earth toilets that had been put in at the end of the platform, shielded by a curtain. There were only six toilets, so the queue was long. Ellie didn't like going to the earth toilets; they stank, so she did her best to wait until they got home.

Ellie and her family and Mrs Watson joined the mass of people trudging up the long, winding staircase. Outside, the smell of burning filled Ellie's nostrils, as it always did when they came out into daylight after sheltering from a night's bombing.

As they walked through the streets towards their house, Ellie wondered if it would still be there. So many buildings had been damaged during the night. The front of one house had fallen into the road, making a pile of rubble and broken bricks they had to scramble over. Ellie looked at the house, which looked like a doll's house with the front removed: downstairs there was a table laid for a meal, with food still on the plates. The people who lived there must have been having their supper when the air-raid siren sounded, and they'd just left everything and run for shelter. Upstairs, the bath was hanging over a large hole in the wooden floor, held in place by the pipe to the taps. If that pipe breaks, the bath will crash down and water will pour everywhere, realised Ellie. That's another family without a home to go to. But at least they escaped before the bombs fell.

They turned the corner into their street, and Ellie was relieved to see their house was still standing. All the houses in the short terrace were untouched.

"We were lucky," said Mum, as she unlocked the door of their house.

To her relief, Ellie was finally able to get to the toilet. When she came back into the kitchen, she found her mum looking in the food cupboard.

"We're out of sugar," sighed Mum. "And we need some margarine as well. Ellie, can you go to Robertson's and get some, please?" She handed Ellie some money, and also her ration book. "There's enough coupons for a pound of sugar and 12 ounces of margarine. That'll get us through the week. And take Micky with you."

"Can we have some sweets?" asked Micky, hopefully. Mum shook her head.

"We've used up all our sweet coupons," she said. "I'll make some sugared bread when you get back."

That's another bad thing about this war, thought Ellie, as she and Micky walked to Robertson's the grocers: *rationing.* Food was in short supply, so at the start of 1940, the government had given orders that people could only have a certain amount of food.

Everyone was issued with a ration book containing a certain number of coupons, with the date on each. You still had to pay for the food, but almost everything was limited to what you had coupons for. Today, Ellie had coupons to get sugar and margarine for the week. Ellie would have preferred butter to margarine, but Mum chose margarine because she could get 12 ounces of margarine with one coupon, but only eight ounces of butter. Margarine was greasier than butter. Ellie had been told by Mrs Watson that this was because it was made from oil from whales, which was also why it had a bit of a fishy taste.

"When the war's over, we'll have butter again," her mum had promised her. But this war seemed like it would never be over.

Chapter 4

Ellie and Micky stood at the counter in the shop and Micky watched enviously as a boy of about his age bought some chocolate.

"Why can't we have sweets?" he asked sulkily.

"Because we have to wait until we can use our next lot of sweet coupons," said Ellie.

"Why do we have to have coupons to buy things if we've got the money to buy them?" demanded Micky.

"Because of the war," replied Ellie. "There's lots of things that we're short of because we don't make them in this country, so they have to come in from other countries. But because the German submarines fire torpedoes at the ships bringing things to us and sink them, the ships can't come over very often."

"Why can't we make sweets in this country?" demanded Micky.

"We do, but sweets need things like chocolate and sugar, and they have to come from abroad. So, there aren't enough sweets to go around. That's why we need coupons. It's a fair way of making sure that everyone gets some," said Ellie. "But when we get home, Mum will make you some sugared bread."

"It's not as good as sweets," grumbled Micky.

Their shopping done, Ellie and Micky were heading home when they met Dolly Rix, a friend of Ellie's from school.

"You weren't at the shelter last night," said Ellie. "I wondered where you were."

"It was Gran," sighed Dolly. "She fell and twisted her ankle, so she couldn't walk."

"We wouldn't have been able to carry her down the stairs to the platforms, so we put her in a pushchair and went round the corner to Mr Feinstein's. He's got a cellar where he and his wife go every night. He helped us get Gran down the steps to the cellar."

Mr Feinstein's was a shop that sold second-hand furniture, clothes, and kitchen stuff like pots and pans and knives and forks.

"It doesn't sound as safe as the tube station," commented Ellie.

"It was safer than trying to get Gran there," said Dolly. She frowned. "Someone broke the windows of Mr Feinstein's shop yesterday. They threw a brick through them."

"Why would anyone do that?" asked Ellie, bewildered. "He's never hurt anyone."

"I don't know," said Dolly. "Anyway, I said I'd get my cousin Bert to give him a hand to board up his windows. I'm on my way to see Bert now, after I've been to Robertson's to do the shopping for my mum."

"Are you getting sweets?" asked Micky, hopefully.

Dolly laughed. "No chance! Not till we can use our next coupons."

Chapter 5

When Ellie got home, she told her mum what she'd heard from Dolly about Mr Feinstein's windows being broken.

"Poor man," sighed her mum. "And his wife, Greta. Such a lovely couple. They had a really hard time of it before they came here."

"Where did they come from?" asked Ellie.

"They were refugees from Germany," said Mum. "They had to leave because they're Jewish, and Hitler and his crowd were making life bad for Jewish people. Smashing up their shops and houses. The Feinsteins left the country after this crowd of Nazis smashed up their shop and took away Greta's younger brother who was working there. He was only 18. It was in a city called Munich."

"What happened to her brother?" asked Ellie.

"They don't know. He never came back. They think he was either locked up in prison, or killed. They couldn't find out."

"Did Mr Feinstein tell you all this?" asked Ellie.

"No," replied Mum. "Greta did. Mr Feinstein never talks about it. Greta said that after that, they couldn't stay in Germany any longer.

So, they packed everything up and came here. That was two years ago. They're good people. Having their windows broken like that must have brought back all those bad memories of what had happened in Munich."

"I thought I'd go and see how they are," said Ellie. "I'll ask them if I can help in any way."

"That's a nice thought," said Mum. "Take Sammy with you."

"Why?" asked Ellie.

"Because he mopes all the time. Going out in the fresh air will do him good."

It won't do me any good, thought Ellie. *All he'll do is moan.* But she took him anyway.

"Where are we going?" asked Sammy.

"To see Mr Feinstein."

"Why?"

"Because someone broke his windows."

"During the air raid?" asked Sammy.

"No. During the day." She shook her head. "Why would anyone do a thing like that?"

"Maybe it's because he's German," said Sammy.

Ellie stopped and looked at him. "What made you say that?" she asked.

"I heard this girl say it at school," said Sammy. "It was in the playground. I heard her talking about the Feinsteins and saying we ought to pay them back for what the Germans were doing."

"But Mr Feinstein isn't German!" exclaimed Ellie.

"This girl said he was," said Sammy.

"Who is this girl?"

"I don't know her name," said Sammy. "She's in a different class to me. She's in Miss Morris's class."

"Do you know where she lives?"

Sammy shook his head, then he said: "If he's German, then Mr Feinstein's our enemy, isn't he?"

"No," said Ellie, firmly. "He and his wife had to leave Germany after their shop was smashed up. They came here to be safe."

"They're not very safe now with the bombing going on every night," commented Sammy.

When they arrived at Mr Feinstein's shop, they found Dolly's cousin, Bert, helping Mr Feinstein to nail boards across the broken windows.

"Hello, Ellie! Sammy!" Bert greeted them cheerfully. "You heard what happened?"

"Yes," said Ellie. She saw Mrs Feinstein appear at the door, a worried look on her face.

"Who could do such a thing?" asked Mrs Feinstein, plaintively.

"Ellie thinks it was a girl from my school," said Sammy.

The Feinsteins and Bert looked at Sammy in surprise, then at Ellie.

"What makes you think that?" asked Bert.

"I didn't say that," said Ellie, defensively.

Then she nodded. "But it may be. Sammy heard a girl at his school saying you were Germans and you were our enemies. She talked about paying you back for the Germans bombing us."

"But we are not your enemies!" burst out Mrs Feinstein. Then she started to cry. "If you knew how we'd suffered!"

Mr Feinstein put his arm around his wife and hugged her to him. "Calm, Greta," he said gently. "If it is this girl, there must be a reason."

"Who is this girl?" asked Bert.

"We don't know," said Ellie. "All Sammy knows is she's in Miss Morris's class at his school."

"My niece, Alice, is in Miss Morris's class," said Bert. He put the hammer back in his tool bag. "We'll get to the bottom of this right now. Alice'll be home in a moment. We'll see if she knows anything about this girl. We'll be back soon, Mr Feinstein, and we'll finish the windows then."

Chapter 6

Bert's niece, Alice, was playing hopscotch on
the pavement outside her house with a friend, when
Bert, Ellie and Sammy appeared.

"Hello, Alice," smiled Bert.

"Hello, Uncle Bert. If you want Mum, she's gone to
see Grandad."

"No, it was you we wanted to talk to."

"Oh?" said Alice, intrigued. "What about?"
She looked at Sammy and said: "I know you. You're in
Miss Boyd's class at our school."

"I am," said Sammy.

"We want to ask you about a girl in your class," said Bert.

"Who?" asked Alice.

"We don't know her name, but Sammy here heard her saying things about Germans. That they ought to pay for what they're doing."

"Oh, you mean Vera Wilson," said Alice. "She hates all Germans."

"Because of the bombing?" asked Bert.

Alice shook her head. "They killed her dad at Dunkirk. Vera's never been the same since it happened."

Bert looked at Ellie and Sammy. "It sounds like it was her who did it," he said.

"Did what?" asked Alice.

"Put a brick through the windows of Mr Feinstein's shop. I've been round there mending it."

"You're helping them? But they're Germans!" said Alice, outraged.

"They're actually Jews and they were chased out of Germany by Hitler and his Nazi crowd," said Ellie.

"Yeh, they're good people," said Bert. "Your friend Vera's got it wrong about them."

"She's not my friend," said Alice, defiantly. "She's just a girl in my class." She looked at her uncle and frowned. "If it was her, what are you going to do about it?"

"I don't know," admitted Bert. "It needs thinking about. Do you know where she lives?"

"23 Plender Street."

"Right," said Bert. "Thanks for that, Alice. And say hello to your mum when she comes back."

As Ellie and Bert walked away, Ellie asked him: "What should we do?"

"I don't know," admitted Bert, unhappily. "By rights we ought to tell the police, but we don't know for sure it was her. It's just suspicion. And the Wilsons will blame us if it turns out not to be her." He gave an unhappy sigh. "I'm not sure what we ought to do, Ellie. But I guess we've got to tell Mr and Mrs Feinstein what we've heard so they can be on their guard."

Chapter 7

Mr and Mrs Feinstein stood and listened as Bert and Ellie told them about Vera Wilson.

"But we don't have any proof it was her," said Bert. "It could have been a relative or a friend of hers."

"No," said Mrs Feinstein. "It's her. I've seen a young girl standing looking at our shop lately from the other side of the road, with such an expression of hate on her face. I didn't know what it was about, or who she was."

"You didn't tell me," protested her husband.

"I didn't like to worry you," said Mrs Feinstein.

"I shall go and see her," said Mr Feinstein.

"Do you think that's a good idea?" asked Bert, concerned. "Remember, the Germans killed her dad: that's what this is all about. You could end up being attacked, not just by Vera, but by her family. And their neighbours. You could get hurt."

"I've been attacked and hurt before," said Mr Feinstein. "But in Munich we could say nothing. It's different here. People have been friendly to us. People like you and your family, Bert. And yours, Ellie."

"But not Vera Wilson," said Ellie.

"No," agreed Mr Feinstein. "That's why I have to go and see her. And her family. To explain who we are, and that we did not kill her father."

"I doubt if they'll listen to you," said Bert.

"I shall try," said Mr Feinstein.

"It's dangerous, Sol," said Mrs Feinstein. "You can't defend yourself against a whole lot of angry people."

"I'll go with you," offered Bert.

"So will I," said Ellie. "They might be less likely to attack you if we're there."

"No," said Mr Feinstein, firmly. "You've done enough already. If you join in, they'll likely seek revenge on you. We can't have that. This is for us to deal with."

"Then I'll go with you," said Mrs Feinstein.

"No," repeated Mr Feinstein. "We both suffered in Munich, but you more than me. I will not let that happen here." He turned to Bert and Ellie. "Thank you for what you've done, Bert. I'll be grateful if you can finish boarding up the windows. And I hope my visit to the Wilsons will mean it won't happen again."

While Bert went back to fixing the boards over the windows, Mr Feinstein put on his coat, kissed his wife, and then set off. Ellie hesitated, unsure what to do, then set off after him, but keeping a good distance from him and ready to dodge out of sight if he turned to look back.

Mr Feinstein reached Plender Street and walked along it until he came to number 23. Ellie was able to find a hiding place behind a van that was parked in the street from where she could watch the Wilson's house unobserved.

Mr Feinstein knocked at the door. After a while, it opened and a middle-aged woman looked out at him.

"Mrs Wilson?" asked Mr Feinstein.

Mrs Wilson glared at him. "What do you mean, knocking on my door, you dirty German!" she spat angrily.

"I am not German," said Feinstein, calmly. "I was born in Russia, but my family were forced to leave Russia and move to Germany when I was a child because we were Jews, and the people in our village didn't want Jews. Yes, I lived in Germany, until the Nazis smashed up our shop and my wife's brother disappeared, and my wife and I were once again forced to leave. I am no German. I am no Nazi. Neither is my wife. We are Jewish. We came to Britain for sanctuary because we thought we would be welcome here. Or, if not welcome, at least we would not be attacked as we were in Russia and Germany. But yesterday, your daughter threw bricks through the windows of our shop ..."

"Oh no, you don't!" shouted Mrs Wilson. "Don't you come here with your lying accusations!"

"She was seen," said Mr Feinstein, still calm. "I know why she did it. The Germans killed her father, and she thinks because I came from Germany that I am German and the enemy. The people who smashed up our shop in Munich were Nazis. Not all Germans are Nazis. There are many Germans who loathe and despise Hitler and everything he stands for. Most of them have been forced to leave Germany, like my wife and myself."

"I would like you to explain this to your daughter and ask her not to attack us. We are not your enemy. We are all victims of the Nazis."

Mrs Wilson stood, silent, looking at Mr Feinstein. Finally, she said: "We didn't know. That you were Jewish."

"There was no reason for you to know," said Mr Feinstein. "Will you talk to your daughter?"

"Yes," said Mrs Wilson. She put her hand on the door, ready to push it shut, then she stopped. "I'm sorry," she said. "It wasn't Vera's fault. She listened to things I said. I didn't know. I was wrong."

"Thank you," said Mr Feinstein.

Mrs Wilson hesitated again, then she asked nervously: "Will you report what happened to the police?"

"No," said Mr Feinstein. "There is no need for them to be involved. You have listened to me and said you will talk to your daughter. That is enough. I'll go now and mend my windows."

"Do you want me to pay for them?" asked Mrs Wilson.

"No," said Mr Feinstein. "You are a widow with a daughter to bring up. I won't take your money. Just your promise that it won't happen again."

"It won't," said Mrs Wilson. "You have my promise."

"Thank you," said Mr Feinstein.

Mrs Wilson hesitated again, then said: "We ought to shake hands on it. The promise, that is. It's what my husband used to do when he gave a promise."

"Thank you," said Mr Feinstein. "I will be honoured to do that."

He held out his hand. Mrs Wilson took it and they shook hands. Then Mr Feinstein nodded in goodbye and left, and Mrs Wilson shut her door.

Chapter 8

It was later that afternoon when there was a knock on the door of Ellie's house. Ellie opened it and was surprised to see Mr and Mrs Feinstein standing there.

"Good afternoon, Ellie," said Mr Feinstein. "Is your mother in?"

"Who is it, Ellie?" called Mum, coming from the kitchen where she was making their supper in case the bombing started earlier than normal. Sammy and Micky followed her.

"Oh, Mr and Mrs Feinstein," said Mum. "I heard what happened to your shop. Ellie told me. That was terrible!"

"But luckily it's all sorted out now," smiled Mr Feinstein. "Thanks to your Ellie. It was she who worked out who caused the trouble, and we have now sorted out our differences. We've come to say thank you."

"Actually, it was Sammy who led us to the girl who did it," said Ellie.

"Indeed," smiled Mr Feinstein. "We have Sammy to thank for his good detective work. And he deserves a reward."

"Here," said Mrs Feinstein, and from her bag she took a ration coupon. "A coupon for sweets."

"And since a coupon needs money as well, here you are," said Mr Feinstein, and he handed Sammy a silver coin.

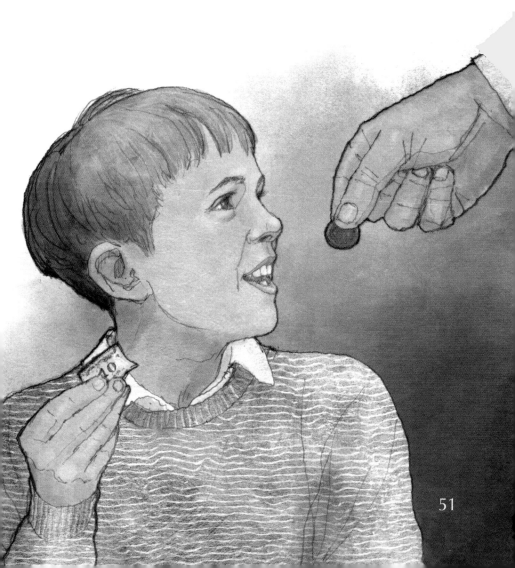

"A shilling!" exclaimed Micky in delight.
"Wow! Sweets!"

Mum hesitated, tempted to tell Sammy to give the coupon and money back, but she saw the looks of happiness on Sammy's and Micky's faces that she hadn't seen for a very long while.

"Make sure you share them with Ellie and Micky," she told Sammy, sternly.

That night in the shelter of the platform at the tube station, as the bombs again rained down outside, Ellie made herself comfortable on the cushions and smiled to herself as she watched Sammy take a piece of chocolate from the paper bag and give it to Micky, before putting a piece into his own mouth.

It had been a good day, thought Ellie. Sammy was happy. Micky was happy. Mr and Mrs Feinstein were happy. And Mrs Wilson and Vera were no longer hating the Feinsteins. And one day soon this war would be over, and her dad would come home and they'd all be together.

And with those comforting thoughts swirling around inside her head, she closed her eyes and – for the first time in a very, very long time – Ellie Smith slept.

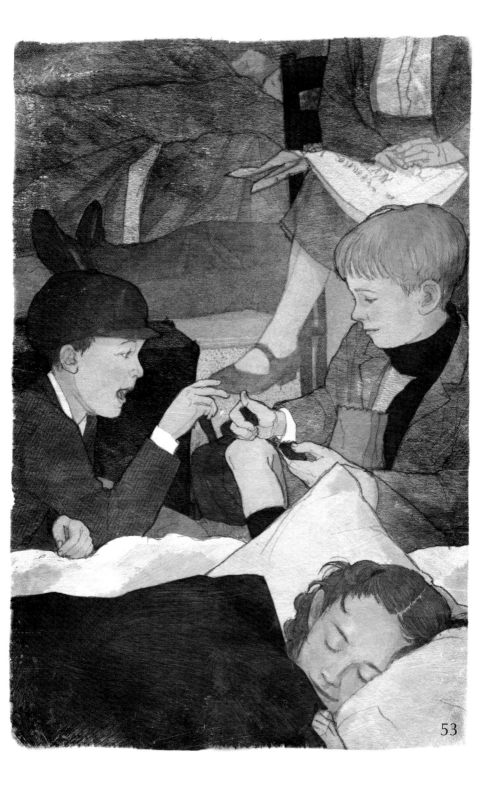

Ellie's Diary

Saturday 28th September 1940

Bombing again. A hundred people sleeping
on the platforms in the tube station.
Tonight, we're near the earth toilets.
It may be convenient, but the smell
is awful! I can't sleep. Mum says
it's because I worry too much, but
there's a lot to worry about. How can
I keep my little brothers, Sammy and
Micky, safe? Will our house still be there
in the morning? I worry about Dad. I miss
him so much. I wish he was home. Is he
being bombed in Egypt? Will this terrible
war ever end?

<u>Sunday 29th September 1940</u>

What a strange day it's been! So much has happened since we were here at the shelter last night.

I'm glad we found out who had been attacking Mr and Mrs Feinstein's shop. And I'm glad they don't have to worry any more. After everything that happened to them in Munich, that's a very good thing. It may be awful missing Dad and worrying about the bombing every night but at least I know where my little brothers are: right here next to me, eating chocolate!

Ideas for reading

Written by Gill Matthews
Primary Literacy Consultant

Reading objectives:

- check that the book makes sense to them, discussing their understanding and exploring the meaning of words in context
- draw inferences such as inferring characters' feelings, thoughts and motives from their actions, and justify inferences with evidence
- participate in discussions about books, building on their own and others' ideas and challenging views courteously

Spoken language objectives:

- maintain attention and participate actively in collaborative conversations, staying on topic and initiating and responding to comments
- participate in discussions, presentations, performances, role play, improvisations and debates

Curriculum links: History – A study of an aspect or theme in British history that extends pupils' chronological knowledge beyond 1066

Interest words: ration book, coupons, pound, ounces, rationing

Resources: ICT; books about the Second World War.

Build a context for reading

- Ask children to look at the front cover of the book. Explore their existing knowledge of the Second World War and the Blitz.
- Ask how the people on the front cover might be feeling and where they could be going.
- Read the blurb. Discuss why someone might be attacking local people.

Understand and apply reading strategies

- Read pp2–4 aloud, asking children to focus on how this first chapter makes them feel. Discuss their responses.
- Explore children's thoughts about how the author starts the story – with action and drama.